Cute and Cuddly: Baby Animals

# PIGLETS

By Grace Elora

Gareth Stevens Publishing

**Please visit our Web site, www.garethstevens.com. For a free color catalog of all our high-quality books, call toll free 1-800-542-2595 or fax 1-877-542-2596.**

**Library of Congress Cataloging-in-Publication Data**

Elora, Grace.
Piglets / Grace Elora.
p. cm. — (Cute and cuddly—baby animals)
ISBN 978-1-4339-4515-1 (library binding)
ISBN 978-1-4339-4516-8 (pbk.)
ISBN 978-1-4339-4517-5 (6-pack)
1. Piglets—Juvenile literature. I. Title.
SF395.5.E46 2011
636.4'07—dc22

2010035611

First Edition

Published in 2011 by
**Gareth Stevens Publishing**
111 East 14th Street, Suite 349
New York, NY 10003



Editor: Therese Shea
Designer: Andrea Davison-Bartolotta

Photo credits: Cover, pp. 3, 5, 7, 9, 15, 17, 19, 21, 24 (all) Shutterstock.com; p. 1 iStockphoto.com; p. 11 Thinkstock.com; p. 13 Image Source/Getty Images; p. 23 Tatyana Makeyeva/AFP/Getty Images.



Printed in the United States of America

CPSIA Compliance Information: Batch #CR217260GS: For further information contact Gareth Stevens, New York, New York at 1-800-542-2595.

# PIGLETS

A baby pig is a piglet.

The mother pig is
a sow.

Sows and piglets stay together.

A piglet has four little legs.

Each foot has four toes.

Some piglets have curly tails. Some have straight tails.

A piglet has a long nose. Its nose finds food!

Mud keeps piglets cool.
Mud keeps bugs away.

Piglets like water. They can swim!

Piglets are smart. They learn tricks!

# Words to Know

curly

sow

straight